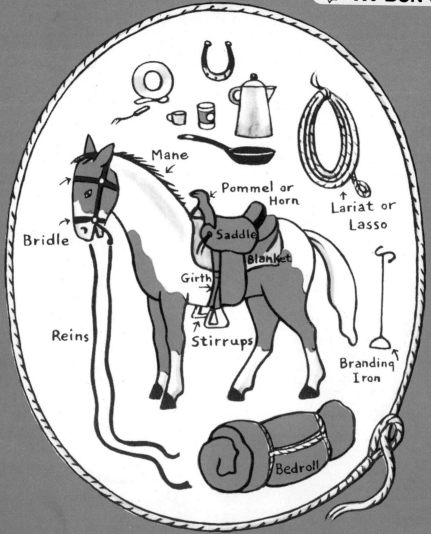

Mane

Pommel or Horn

Lariat or Lasso

Bridle

Saddle

Blanket

Girth

Reins

Stirrups

Branding Iron

Bedroll

Books to Read Aloud

The Big Golden Book of Poetry	edited by Jane Werner
Finders Keepers	Will and Nicolas
Little Frightened Tiger	Golden MacDonald
The Man Who Didn't Wash His Dishes	Phyllis Krasilovsky
The Old Woman and Her Pig	illustrated by Paul Galdone
Rosa-Too-Little	Sue Felt
Six Foolish Fishermen	retold by Benjamin Elkin
The Three Billy Goats Gruff	P. C. Asbjørnsen and J. E. Moe
Umbrella	Taro Yashima
Where Does the Butterfly Go When It Rains	May Garelick

Books to Enrich the Content Fields

The Big Book of Real Fire Engines	illustrated by George Zaffo
The Listening Walk	Paul Showers
One Snail and Me	Emilie McLeod
The Sky Was Blue	Charlotte Zolotow
What Is A Turtle	Gene Darby

Books for Independent Reading

Belling the Cat and Other Stories	retold by Leland Jacobs
Big Talk	Miriam Schlein
Cowboy Small	Lois Lenski
Gertie the Duck	Nicholas Georgiady and Louis Romano
Indian Two Feet and His Horse	Margaret Friskey
Josie and the Snow	Helen Buckley
Karen's Opposites	A. and M. Provensen
Millions and Millions and Millions!	Louis Slobodkin
Nothing but Cats, Cats, Cats	Grace Skaar
Robins and Rabbits	John Hawkinson

Cowboy Small

by
Lois Lenski

Henry Z. Walck, Inc.

New York

Special Scott, Foresman and Company Edition
for the *Invitations to Personal Reading* Program

bedroll—blankets rolled up
bit—metal bar in horse's mouth
bridle—straps around horse's head, with bit and reins
brand—a mark
bronco—wild horse, not used to a rider
bucking—kicking, with head between front legs
bunk—bed
bunkhouse—house for cowboys' beds
chaps—overalls of leather, open at the back
chuckwagon—wagon that carries food and bedrolls
                for cowboys
corral—a fenced-in yard for cows or horses
curries—scrapes the horse's hide with a currycomb
dismounts—gets down
girth—strap around the body of the horse,
             to hold the saddle in place
mounts—gets up
ranch—a large farm with grass for cows
range—open place where cows eat grass
reins—straps used to drive a horse
saddle—seat for rider, made of leather
stirrup—loop at end of strap hung from saddle,
             to hold foot of rider

This edition is printed and distributed by Scott, Foresman and
Company by special arrangement with Henry Z. Walck, Inc.,
19 Union Square West, New York, N. Y. 10003.

Cowboy Small

"Hi, there!"
calls
Cowboy Small.

Cowboy Small
has a horse.
His name is Cactus.
He keeps him in the barn
at Bar S Ranch.

Cowboy Small
takes good care
of Cactus.
He brushes him and curries him.

He feeds him
oats and hay.

He gives him water
to drink.

Cowboy Small
puts the saddle on.
He pulls the girth tight.

"Whoa, Cactus!"

Cowboy Small
puts his left foot
in the stirrup
and mounts.

"Giddap, Cactus!"

Cowboy Small rides out
on the range.
Cloppety, cloppety, clop!

"Whoa, Cactus!"

Cowboy Small
dismounts.
He fixes the fence.

Cowboy Small makes camp
for the night.
He cooks supper and eats it.
Oh, how good it tastes!

Cowboy Small rolls up
in his bedroll.
He goes to sleep
under the stars.

Next morning,
Cowboy Small rides in the Bar S roundup.

The cowboys round up all the cows.
"Yip-pee! Yip-pee! Yip-pee!"

"Come and get it!"
calls the cook at noon.

Cowboy Small
eats at the chuckwagon
with the cowboys.
They have beef,
red beans and coffee.

"Yip-pee!
Ride 'em, cowboy!"

Cowboy Small
ropes a calf
in the corral.

Cowboy Small helps
with the branding.
The calves are marked
with the Bar S brand:

S̄

Cowboy Small
turns the cows back
on the range.

At night,
Cowboy Small
plays his guitar
and sings:

"Home . . .
        home on the range . . ."

He goes to sleep
in the bunkhouse.

Next day,
Cowboy Small
rides a bucking bronco.

"Yip-pee! —Yip-pee!
Ride 'em, cowboy!"

Ker-plop!

Cowboy Small
hits
the
dust!

But—

he's a pretty good cowboy,
after all!
Cactus is waiting,

so—

"Giddap, Cactus!"

Cowboy Small
rides
again!

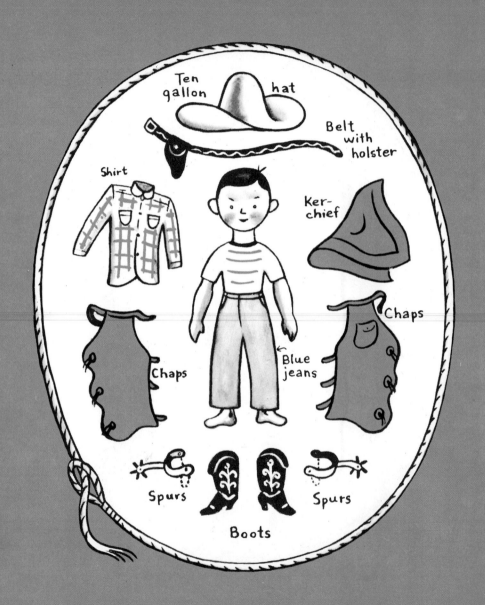